DOUGLAS

For Mom

◆ ◆ ◆

First edition 2019

Library of Congress Catalog Card Number pending
ISBN 978-0-7636-3397-4

19 20 21 22 23 24 CCP 10 9 8 7 6 5 4 3 2 1

Printed in Shenzhen, Guangdong, China

This book was typeset in Filosofia.
The illustrations were done in oil.

Candlewick Press
99 Dover Street
Somerville, Massachusetts 02144

visit us at www.candlewick.com

DOUGLAS

RANDY CECIL

CANDLEWICK PRESS

ACT I

· 1 ·

On a Saturday afternoon in Bloomville,
Iris Espinosa put on her sister's blue sweater
and stepped out the front door.
A familiar buttery scent wafted through the air.

Popcorn.

Iris headed down the steps . . .

and made her way along the sidewalk,
past the enormous cat with six toes on each paw . . .

past Everett Dunn, whose mother did not allow him
to go beyond his stoop alone . . .

to the Majestic Cinema, where she bought a small box of popcorn
from a street vendor and a ticket from the box office.
Then she stepped inside.

She made her way down the aisle
and along the front row to her usual seat.

The lights dimmed, and the projector started up
with a *click, click, click.*
Iris watched the screen, rapt, as her hero leapt and dashed about,
narrowly escaping danger at every turn.

· 2 ·

A few rows back, a little mouse was watching the screen, too.

But the sight of popcorn falling through the fingers of
the Woman with the Large Hat a few seats over
pulled the little mouse away.

The Woman with the Large Hat came to the cinema every afternoon.
And, to the little mouse's delight,
she happened to be very careless with her snacks.

The little mouse danced about,
snatching falling kernels from the air . . .

and feasting on one fluffy bite after another,
until she felt rather queasy.

To ease her aching belly, the little mouse took a little walk.
And she belched a little belch.
Then she hopped up on a cushiony seat to take a nap.

To her surprise, a girl in a blue sweater was sitting
in the next seat over, smiling at her.

The little mouse considered skittering away.
But her belly was still rumbling. So she settled down
in the soft, cozy folds of the girl's sweater instead.

On the screen, the hero was bravely swinging on
a vine from one castle window to another.
But the little mouse was more interested in a pocket she had
discovered above the folds of the girl's blue sweater.
The pocket looked like the softest, coziest place of all.
So she climbed inside.
Then the little mouse fell asleep.

· 3 ·

When the little mouse awoke, she poked her head out of the pocket
and found that she was outside, in the brilliant light of day,
for the first time in her life.

Her eyes widened at the wonder of it all.

But then she saw an unsettling sight.
An enormous beast with six toes on each paw
was sprawled, half asleep, across a stoop.

And even more unsettling, the beast woke suddenly
and sniffed at the air. Then it pulled itself up off the stoop
and began to follow her.

Block after block, the beast lumbered along behind her,
watching her and licking its lips . . .

until finally, to the little mouse's great relief,
the Girl in the Blue Sweater climbed a stoop, opened a door,
and left the street and the beast behind.

When Iris reached her bedroom, she took off her sister's sweater
and hung it on the doorknob. Then she sat down on the
edge of the bed with the last of her popcorn.

But to her surprise, just as she was about to pop the last kernel
into her mouth, the little mouse from the cinema
poked its head out of the sweater pocket.

It leapt to the floor, twitched its nose, and sniffed at the air.
Then, spotting the kernel of popcorn in Iris's hand, it leapt from
a stack of books, up onto a stool, and over to the bed.

The little mouse's daring reminded Iris of her favorite actor,
Douglas Fairbanks. So she decided to name the little mouse Douglas.

Iris said the name aloud. "Douglas."
And the little mouse's eyes seemed to sparkle.

As Douglas nibbled the last kernel of popcorn, Iris dressed the little mouse
in a dashing vest taken from one of her dolls. Then she sat back to admire
her work. *Just like Douglas Fairbanks*, she thought.

Then she heard her sister stomping down the hallway.
So she quickly slipped Douglas out of sight.

A moment later, the bedroom door swung open,
and Iris's annoyed sister reclaimed her sweater.

· 5 ·

The girl exiting the apartment was not the same one the Six-Toed Cat had
watched enter. But the blue sweater was the same. And, more important,
so was the little mouse poking its head out of one of the pockets.

So the old Six-Toed Cat picked himself up off the sidewalk
and followed them.

Block after block, he watched as the little mouse tried to hide deep
in the sweater pocket, only to poke its head out again a moment later
to see that the Six-Toed Cat was still following.
But of course he was.

· 6 ·

Adriana Espinosa was meeting her boyfriend's mother, Mrs. Hubbard,
for the first time, and she wanted everything to be perfect.
So she checked her hair, then gathered her nerves and rang the buzzer.

Winston opened the door and smiled.
And together they made their way up a flight of stairs.

A moment later, Adriana was smiling and nodding politely
as Winston made introductions.

This is going so well, thought Adriana as they all sat down for a cup of tea in the living room. And then she sneezed.

She reached her hand into her sweater pocket,
hoping to find a handkerchief.
Instead she felt something furry. And whiskery.

It wriggled in her hand.

Adriana screamed and screamed
as she flung the furry thing across the room.

· 7 ·

When her head stopped spinning, Douglas found herself
high atop a bookcase. She stood frozen as, all around her,
people screamed and teacups rattled.

But when a woman wielding a broom charged toward her,
Douglas sprang into action.

She leapt from the bookcase to a curtain . . .

and swung on the curtain out a window and onto a ledge.

Then she shimmied across the ledge to the corner of the building,
where she pulled herself upward, little by little . . .

until she reached the roof.

Exhausted, Douglas collapsed in a tiny heap on the rooftop.
As her racing heart slowly quieted and her shaking legs slowly stilled,
night began to fall, and the first real stars Douglas had ever seen
appeared in the sky.

She watched as they twinkled, so beautiful yet so impossibly far away.

Then she curled up on the hard rooftop
and fell into an uneasy sleep.

ACT II

1

As the sun rose over Bloomville the next morning,
Douglas awoke and blinked her eyes. Then she climbed to the top
of a nearby chimney and looked out over the town.

Off in the distance, the Majestic Cinema sparkled in the morning sun:
the cinema, where there were no broom-wielding women
or enormous beasts and popcorn fell like rain.

She climbed down the chimney, then skittered to the roof's edge
and peered over. The Beast was staring back up at her.

2

What the Six-Toed Cat had lost in quickness over the years,
he made up for in patience. And after so many years hunting mice,
he knew how they thought. He knew their next moves,
even before they did. He knew this little mouse was on the run.

The Six-Toed Cat picked himself up off the sidewalk and stretched.

Slowly, patiently, he tracked the little mouse
as it ran from rooftop to rooftop.

Each time he spotted the little mouse, it appeared a little more confident
and a little more capable than the last time, leaping a bit higher,
jumping a bit farther, and swinging a bit more gallantly.

After watching his prey leap across an alley, the Six-Toed Cat
knew that this was a mouse that would not give up easily.

But neither would he.

Douglas had, in fact, just barely made the leap across the alley.
Clinging to the roof's edge, she scratched and clawed and pulled herself up.

Then she dusted herself off and continued on, every so often peering over the roof's edge to see if the Beast was still there.

It was.

But on one of these occasions, she saw something else.
Could it be?

Down below, on the sidewalk, stood her friend from the cinema—
the Girl in the Blue Sweater.

Douglas scampered to the corner of the rooftop
and swung over the ledge.

She slid down a drainpipe . . .

then leapt to a trash can and up to a stoop post.

From here, it was just a short dash up the sidewalk to
the Girl in the Blue Sweater and her cozy pocket.

But before she could make her move,
a meaty hand reached out and grabbed her.

· 4 ·

The meaty hand belonged to Everett Dunn.
And the more the little mouse tried to wriggle free,
the tighter his grip became.

Everett had always wanted a pet, but he was not allowed to have one.
A neighbor's dog followed him home one day,

and another neighbor's dog followed him home the next.
After that, his mother had not allowed him to go beyond his stoop alone.

Everett was thrilled to finally have a pet.
And he hadn't had to go beyond the stoop to get it.

· 5 ·

When Henrietta Dunn returned home from a trip to the store, she was
relieved to find her son, Everett, quietly behaving himself in the living room.

Henrietta thought perhaps she had been too hard on him.
After all, he only wanted a pet of his own.

6

Once again, Douglas was flung across a room.
She grabbed hold of the ceiling fan, which spun her around.

And when she let go,
it sent her flying out the window.

She landed atop a trash can, then leapt over a railing
to the sidewalk, and scurried away . . .

across one busy intersection . . .

then another . . .

to an alley, where she hopped and leapt
and pulled herself back up onto another rooftop.

7

Exhausted, Douglas once again collapsed in a tiny heap on the rooftop.

Later, once her heart had stopped racing, she looked up at the sky.
Clouds floated past like giant fluffy kernels of popcorn,
forever beyond her reach.

With her mouth watering and stomach rumbling,
Douglas curled up on the hard rooftop and into a restless sleep.

ACT III

When she awoke, Douglas was amazed to discover that
the Majestic Cinema was closer than she could have dreamed.

She hopped up to the roof's edge and gazed down below.
The Beast was nowhere in sight.

So she hopped back down and began her
triumphant march toward home.

But as she darted along an old, frayed clothesline,
something caught her eye. Down below were not one, not two,
but three young, hungry-looking cats.

The sight so unsettled Douglas that she lost her footing
and fell from the clothesline, grabbing hold of the end of a stocking
just in the nick of time.

For a moment, she dangled high above the ground as the three cats
gathered beneath her, licking their lips.

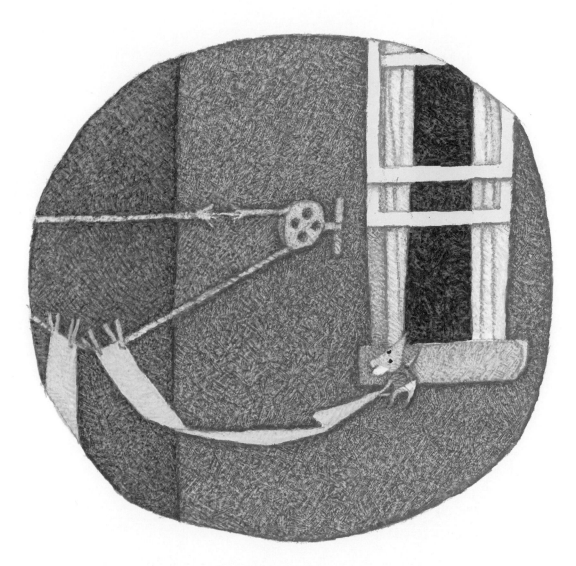

Kicking her legs forward, then back, then forward and back again,

Douglas swung higher and higher.

Each swing brought her closer to the window above.

But each swing also further unraveled the frayed clothesline.

Just as she grabbed hold of the window ledge,
the clothesline snapped and fell to the ground.

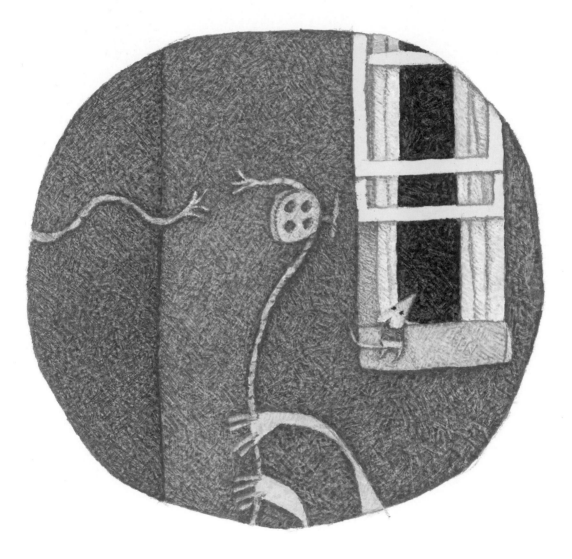

· 2 ·

On the other side of that very window, in an otherwise empty apartment,
another mouse sat nervously clutching a cookie crumb.

Some time ago, when the mouse was just a tiny baby,
he had slipped into the empty apartment underneath the door.

He had followed his nose straight to a kitchen cabinet filled
with long-forgotten food, where, day after day,
he had feasted on dried beans and pasta and cookies.
And each day, the mouse had grown a little bigger and stronger.

When only one cookie crumb remained, the mouse tucked
the crumb under his arm for a later treat and headed out
the way he had entered. Only then did he realize that he had
grown too big to slip back under the door.

So the mouse had hopped up onto a windowsill to look for another way out.
Unfortunately, at that very moment, a terrifying monster happened
to look up and see him standing in the window.

The mouse had quickly jumped back down to the floor.

Later, when he hopped up onto the windowsill again,
there were two monsters looking back at him.

And the third time he hopped up onto the windowsill, there were three.
The mouse couldn't leave his apartment. But he couldn't stay, either.

Clutching his cookie crumb, he had sat down on the empty floor
and wished for a miracle.

Just then, seemingly out of nowhere, a brave-looking mouse
in a dashing vest appeared on the windowsill.

· 3 ·

Douglas's heart went out to the mouse sitting on the floor.
She could see that he was alone and afraid, just as she had been.

She would rescue this mouse in distress!

Douglas leapt from window to window in search of an escape route.
But there was no way up to the roof.

And with the hungry-looking cats patrolling down below,
the sidewalk was out of the question.

So Douglas sat down on the window ledge to think.
That's when things went from bad to worse.

· 4 ·

The Six-Toed Cat approached the three young cats, wary
but determined. He had come too far to give up on this mouse.
Especially now that he finally had it trapped.

5

As the cats raged on, Douglas began to lose any hope of escape. Then the big mouse leapt up onto the windowsill and sat down.

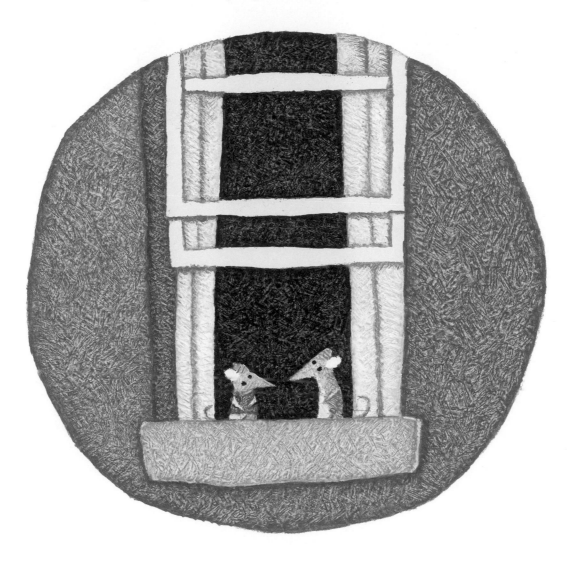

Douglas didn't want the mouse to see the despair in her eyes,
so she looked away. There, in the distance, she saw a familiar sight.

Suddenly she had a plan.

Mrs. Pennington caught her reflection in a store window
and stopped for a moment to adjust her large hat.

Then she continued on,
smiling at everyone she passed.

But her smile faded as she passed a group of cats
hissing angrily at one another.

She turned and faced the cats to show her displeasure at their
unruly behavior. The cats seemed not to even notice her.
So she considered wagging her finger and telling them a thing or two.

The Six-Toed Cat sniffed the air as a gentle breeze blew past.
It caught his attention because nowhere within it
was the scent of mice.

He looked up and saw an empty window where the mice had been.
He looked up the street. And he looked down the street.
But the mice were nowhere to be found.

Suddenly he was lifted into the air. Everett, the same child he had sent
tumbling to the ground, now held him firmly. To his own surprise,
the Six-Toed Cat let out a small purr.

Then, just as suddenly as the Six-Toed Cat had been scooped up
by the child, the child was scooped up by his mother.
And they all headed home together.

ACT IV

· 1 ·

The next Saturday afternoon in Bloomville,
Iris put on her sister's blue sweater
and stepped out the front door.
A familiar buttery scent wafted through the air.

Popcorn.

Iris headed down the steps . . .

and made her way along the sidewalk, past the Six-Toed Cat,
who was climbing onto Everett Dunn's lap and stretching his neck
to show off his brand-new collar . . .

to the cinema, where she bought a small box of popcorn
from a street vendor and a ticket from the box office.
Then she stepped inside.

She made her way down the aisle and along
the front row to her usual seat.
The lights dimmed, and the projector started up
with a *click, click, click.*

Iris could barely contain her excitement
when Douglas leapt up onto the seat next to her
with a new friend.

As she watched the two mice share a kernel of popcorn,
she decided to give Douglas's new friend a name.
"Pearl," she said aloud, thinking of her favorite actress, Pearl White.

The mouse's eyes seemed to sparkle.
And Iris couldn't stop smiling.

· 2 ·

Douglas wanted to return the girl's smile with a smile of her own.
A smile that told what it felt like to be the hero of a grand adventure.
And, even better, to return home from that grand adventure
to soft, cushiony seats and endless fluffy popcorn.

But Douglas was sleepy, so she crawled into
the girl's sweater pocket and snuggled up next to Pearl.

Then she fell asleep.